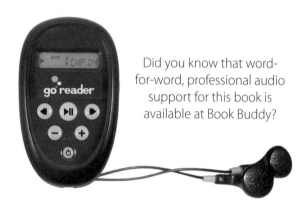

Did you know that word-for-word, professional audio support for this book is available at Book Buddy?

GoReader™ powered by Book Buddy is pre-loaded with word-for-word audio support to build strong readers and achieve Common Core standards.

The corresponding GoReader™ for this book can be found at: http://bookbuddyaudio.com

Or send an email to: info@bookbuddyaudio.com

TALES OF
THE UNCOOL

The Great Geek
REBELLION
of Halsey School

BY KIRSTEN RUE
ILLUSTRATED BY SARA RADKA

The Great Geek Rebellion of Halsey School
Tales of the Uncool

Copyright © 2015

Published by Scobre Educational

Written by Kirsten Rue

Illustrated by Sara Radka

Printed in the United States of America.

Scobre Educational
2255 Calle Clara
La Jolla, CA 92037

Scobre Operations & Administration
42982 Osgood Road
Fremont, CA 94539

www.scobre.com
info@scobre.com

Scobre Educational publications may be purchased for educational, business, or sales promotional use.

Cover and layout design by Jana Ramsay
Copyedited by Renae Reed

ISBN: 978-1-62920-140-5 (Soft Cover)
ISBN: 978-1-62920-139-9 (Library Bound)
ISBN: 978-1-62920-138-2 (eBook)

Table of Contents

The Roar

IT WAS THE TRIP THAT REALLY DID IT. "THE TRIP THAT Started It All," my friend Samantha calls it. I guess she's always had a dramatic side. What happened was this:

I was leaving Computer Resource class. Mrs. Zuck, the computer teacher, has been giving me special projects for the whole year. What I can I say? Computers are just kind of *easy* for me. I left class, but before I did, I helped this other kid—Joe Russo— with the Microsoft Excel spreadsheet he was making.

He grunted, but I couldn't tell if that was supposed to mean "thank you" or what.

I left class, head held high, and *BAM!* All I could feel was the gross school carpet scratching my cheek. What do they have under there, cement?! My arm hurt. My ankle hurt. My glasses had somehow popped off and rolled to an inch away from my nose. (These are really cool glasses, BTW. I got them online.)

Even though I couldn't see anything (duh, no glasses), I could hear laughter. Like, all around. Laughter from above and below. Laughter in every pitch between low and high. Coming down the hall, still echoing as it rounded the curves into other classrooms. I'm pretty sure I heard even Joe Russo's deep, husky chuckle, and heck, I had just been *helping* him. I mean, without me, I highly doubt he would even *pass* Computer Resource class.

As I lay there, I worried just a little bit that the hem of my shirt had ridden up and that other kids walking by might be able to see the waistband of my underwear. They're Hanes, in case you're wondering. I definitely didn't like the idea of Mrs. Zuck seeing them. Ugh. I didn't like that idea at all. I hoped that the scratchy carpet hadn't actually given me a legit rub burn. Because those are annoying.

Mainly, though? I was just really, really mad. I could feel the anger like hot prickles of light alternating with cool prickles. My friends and I, we've been pushed around Halsey School all year. We're anxious about just going into the Freeburger for a shake and

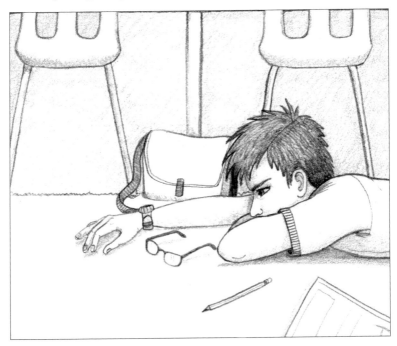

fries because of the looks we get. Even if the other kids don't say anything to our faces, we can hear the whispers. We can see them point and roll their eyes. We get tripped, cheated off of, have our homework ripped out of our hands and torn in half in the hallways. The list goes on. I'm actually afraid of listing any more torture tactics here, because, you know, we don't want to give anyone any ideas . . .

Everyone at school calls us the Doomsday Geeks. I guess they think that we all play Dungeons and Dragons or something. Okay, so Glenn *does* like Dungeons and Dragons and I happen to like a game called Valcora. But what does that have to do with anything? We, as a group, are going places. We win every Science Fair and turn in our homework on time—no, *early*—every week. I think we're nice enough guys (and a couple of girls . . . yes, girls, I'm serious). And yet it doesn't matter how much we keep a low profile or avoid making eye contact with the Football Lardos and the Deadly Sweets. We just can't win.

This time, though? I had had it. I pushed myself up from the carpet and I roared. I'm serious. An actual, honest-to-goodness, "*Roooooooaaarrrr!!!*"

The laughter stopped. Samantha, my friend, stood next to me and crossed her arms, like, "Don't mess with us." I heard Pete Russo whisper the word "Weirdo!" to his friend Tom Zellingersburgerzing. (Okay, that's not his real name. *Nobody* knows how to spell his real name.)

One of the Sweets (the most dreaded, most popular girls in school) took out her phone and started texting at lightning speed. A couple of teachers popped their heads out of their classroom doors. One was Mrs. Zuck, and when I made eye contact with her, I could tell that she kind of understood. Like she always says, she grew up in love with computers when all girls were supposed to love horses and sparkle pens. She gets it.

There were gasps as a short, determined figure began huffing and puffing up the hallway. The crowd parted to either side and kids started ducking towards the lunchroom, gym—anywhere—as fast as they could go. I think I was the last person to figure out who it was: Assistant Principal McCloud.

"Did I hear a roar?" Assistant Principal McCloud bellowed. "Who's shouting in the halls?"

I knew Mrs. Zuck would never rat me out. She ducked back into her classroom. None of the other kids made eye contact with McCloud, either. Besides maybe Mrs. Pruggle the math teacher, *no one* is more feared than McCloud. Samantha reached out and touched my arm, trying to get me to back up. But I didn't budge.

"Principal McCloud, sir?" I said loudly, raising my hand. "I shouted. And I did it in protest!"

And that's how the Great Geek Rebellion of Halsey School began.

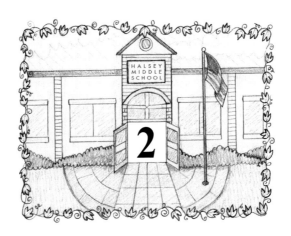

Publicity Campaign

Assistant Principal McCloud was too busy that day to haul me off to his office, but he told me to be there during lunch hour the next day. 12 p.m. sharp.

So, with just a few minutes to go before I have to report for questioning, I stand with my friends, discussing the situation. It's five of us, counting me: Glenn, Samantha, Kirk, and J.D. (Kirk and J.D. are twins, and you pretty much never see them apart. Heck, I can't even *tell* them apart sometimes.) We huddle at

Glenn's locker, which is close to some benches and fake plants.

"Okay, Tim, so you don't want to apologize, right?" Glenn asks.

"Nothing to apologize for," I say. I'm determined.

"Yeah, but we want an *allegiance* with the faculty."

"Geez, Glenn. Stop trying to sound like you're in a movie or something," Samantha cuts in. "I think what he *means,* Tim, is that you don't want McCloud to get mad. We want him to understand our point of view."

"Sure, sure," I say. Not to toot my own horn or anything, but I *am* sort of the boss of this group. Sorta. If you don't ask Samantha. She might think she's the boss.

"But," Glenn says, "you have to come in there with terms . . . proposals . . ."

Samantha holds up her hand to put Glenn on pause. "Seriously, Glenn, you are not in a movie. That is just how it is." Kirk and J.D. laugh.

"You know what we need?" I say, because the idea

has just come to me, and it might be a really good idea.

"What?" Glenn and Samantha say in the same breath.

"A good P.R. campaign."

Now it's Glenn who doesn't get it. "Personal Record?" he asks.

"Nope. P.R. It's like what my Dad always says about working for Zenith—"

"Yeah, Tim," Samantha interrupts, dramatically rolling her eyes. "We get it. Your dad's a programmer at Zenith. Big whoop."

"Yeah, but listen," I try again. "My dad told me this story once. About how everybody was *not* buying Zenith phones. They were buying Filotech phones instead. So, Zenith started having these commercials. They made it seem like 'Filotech phones are boring and lame, but Zenith computers are *unique*. Zenith phones are for cool people.'"

"And your point?" Samantha is definitely one of my best friends, but one thing that drives me crazy about her? She's impatient and rude.

"My *point* is that it worked! Next thing my dad knew, Zenith phones were flying off the shelves. I mean, do any of you even have a Filotech phone?"

Kirk and J.D. pull their phones from their pockets. "No, man," they say. "We convinced our parents to get us the Sprocket." Of course they did.

"Anyway, we're getting off track here," I press on. "The *point* is that those commercials were a *public relations* campaign. They changed people's minds. And that's what we need. We need people to stop seeing us a certain way, and see us in a better way. And then leave us alone!"

"I'm on it," Glenn says. "Samantha and I are on it." Samantha looks annoyed to be volunteered for the job, but she still nods.

"But . . . we didn't cover what you're going to say to McCloud," Kirk points out. "And now it's 11:57."

I've been trying to act cool in front of the others, but actually? My stomach is still nervous and tied up in knots. I've only seen him floating down the hallways like an angry, balled-up cloud. I've never actually had to talk to him before.

"At this point, guys, just get to the lunchroom. The best thing to do is act like everything's normal. They won't even see it coming."

"Who's they?" Samantha asks, but by then, it's too late. The clock turns 11:59 and I rush towards Assistant Principal McCloud's office.

———

BEVERLY, THE WOMAN WHO WORKS AT THE HALSEY FRONT desk, is always really nice. I know because last year I got a piece of gravel stuck in my hand and had to wait to get into the nurse's office. While I waited, she brought me a little plastic cup of juice and half of a donut with sprinkles on top.

"Shhhhh!" she said, her eyes twinkling at me. Even her lipstick kind of looked like crushed-up sugar. "These are left over from the staff meeting this morning!" I remember being annoyed that the teachers

and principals get to have donuts while *we* have the gross "Halsey Meat Bar." But I couldn't be mad at Beverly. I wish, today, that she didn't have to see me waiting to go into McCloud's office. It doesn't really help with my whole idea of making our image better.

"Mr. Watkins," she says, looking up with a little disappointed frown. "Mr. McCloud will see you now."

The door to McCloud's office is made out of dark, gleaming wood. It makes it seem like he's the warlord of a huge castle or something like that. (Okay, so in my game, Valcora, there are a lot of warlords in castles.) I creep up to it and knock very lightly on the heavy wood. Silence. I knock again.

"Come in!" McCloud says, and as I push the door open, it creeeaaakksss on its hinges.

———

ASSISTANT PRINCIPAL MCCLOUD'S OFFICE IS FULL OF PHOTOS of fish. I didn't expect that. There's a huge picture of a swordfish on the wall behind his desk, fish figurines all over his bookshelf, and even a framed photo on the wall . . . of? You guessed it: McCloud holding a huge fish in his fists, smiling a wide smile. He also has a little goldfish bowl where a sparkly yellow fish with floaty fins stares out at the room, probably looking directly at me.

"Mr. Watkins," McCloud says, "take a seat."

I sit across from him, trying not to be distracted by the floaty yellow fish that is staring at me for sure.

McCloud leans his elbows on the desk and plops his chin in his hands. "Now tell me about this roar."

"Well, Mr. McCloud, sir," I begin, though once again I'm distracted by the fishbowl. I'm almost certain that McCloud's fish is doing backflips in there.

"Try not to be distracted by Chloe," he says. "That's my fish."

"Right. Well, sir . . . the truth is . . ." *C'mon, Watkins, don't lose your cool now!* "Yesterday, I—I got upset. Well, mad. And so I protested."

"By roaring."

"Right. I just, well, *we*—my friends and I—we just

want some more respect. I was tired of getting pushed around. So I roared."

"Very loudly, I might add," says McCloud. "I heard it all the way in the break room, where I was having my donut." *Do Halsey staff have a constant parade of donuts or something?!*

Up close, and without his fast, angry walk, McCloud still looks stern. Yet he doesn't look mean, exactly. His face is all different colors of pink, purple, and red, and his white hair is thinning on the top of his head. He wears a fat ring on one hand that catches the light and is almost as distracting as Chloe.

"Do you think a roar is really the best way to get your point across?"

"No, sir! So, that's why we're doing things differently. We're going to have a—a campaign. And then, by doing that, hopefully . . ." I trail off. McCloud doesn't seem to be listening. Instead, he's cocked his head to one side, as if he can hear something from the other room that I can't. Maybe the fish talks to him or something.

"You know what I want to see, Mr. Watkins?" he asks. "I want to see that this campaign or *thing* that you're talking about does NOT involve roaring or otherwise causing a distraction at Halsey School. Do you think you and your friends will be able to handle that?"

"Yes, sir. Definitely. We will not bother anybody in the school." *Well, correction, we* might *bother them, but it will be for a good cause. And loud in a good way, too.*

"Good, I'm glad to hear it." Assistant Principal McCloud thumps his fist on his desk. Inside her bowl, Chloe jumps and flutters her fins again.

"Thank you, sir. For not giving me a detention or anything," I say. He simply smiles.

"Just hope I don't have to deal with you again, Mr. Watkins. Remember what I said about distractions." His smile is still frozen on his face, but his eyes definitely DON'T look happy.

"I won't, sir!" I leap up and open the door before he can say anything else, slipping out to the front office in relief. I walk as quickly as I can, my heart pounding in triumph. First problem: Solved. Maybe I'll even be able to make it for the end of lunch!

As I leave, Beverly waves me over with a secretive smile. She slides a pack of Skittles over the top of the counter. "Shhhhh," she says again, with a wink. Beverly is definitely the best thing about Halsey School.

A Plan

B Y THE TIME I SLIDE INTO MY REGULAR SEAT IN THE cafeteria, I really only have time to gulp down a carton of chocolate milk.

"*So???*" the twins ask, leaning over the table. I take my time finishing the milk.

"I think Assistant Principal McCloud is on our side," I say. "I really do."

"He didn't give you a detention or anything?" asks Glenn breathlessly.

"Nope. Nada. He said he just doesn't want us to

create a distraction."

"Were we . . . going to create a distraction?" Glenn's eyes look confused behind his glasses.

"Well . . . I did have some pretty good ideas on the way over here."

"If it's about our publicity campaign, Samantha and I have it covered."

"Yeah," she chimes in. "Let me show you." Samantha pulls out her phone and holds up the screen for me to see.

Happenings at Halsey School, says the screen.

"We're going to make a blog. And I already know who can help us write it."

"Someone we can trust?" I ask. You can't be too careful at Halsey, *especially* when you're dealing with coolness.

"Yeah. That guy Damien who sits at our table."

"Okay, whatever. Cool. That can definitely be part of it. But I think . . . we should go even *bigger*."

"Um," says Kirk. "This won't affect our homework

or anything, right?"

J.D. nods. "Like, I have my after-school violin lessons and we're also working on our applications to NASA camp," J.D. chimes in. Sometimes I feel like I have to do all the work around here.

"Well, here's what I think," I say. I know it can sometimes take some convincing to get the Geeks to think outside the box. And that box is about ninety-eight percent made up of homework and worrying about college. I mean, GEEZ, we have like *years* left to go before college. "I think if we do some work now on our *image*, it means less work later. Like, having to re-do homework after one of the Lardos steals it."

"Or having to go to the bathroom between classes and clean the spit wads off our necks!" Glenn adds.

"Yeah, exactly! I think we should find a way to change our image. So. Here's what I think." I take a deep breath. "I think we should organize a dance."

After I share my idea, the table goes silent. You can hear trays clattering on the metal tray racks in the lunch line. You can even make out the *"Shhhhhh!"* of Ms. Arple, the lunch monitor, as someone raises his voice too high. I mean, I guess I knew I would get a shocked reaction to my idea, but still. This is even more shocked than I expected when I first had my idea, sitting in McCloud's office and on the way to the lunchroom. I feel a little drop of sweat slide down behind my ear. Is it hot in here or what?!

Finally, Samantha breaks the silence. "Whoa, Tim. A dance?! Are you being serious?"

You might think I'm nervous because of the sweat dripping behind my ear, but nope. "I'm one-hundred percent sure," I say back in a brave tone. I figure that's what being a leader is all about, right? If *I* think it's the best idea in the world, I have to make sure my friends see it that way, too. I need their support, after all.

I can tell I have my work cut out for me in convincing the others, though. Kirk and J.D. are just quiet, their matching mouths slightly open. Glenn has turned a pretty bright shade of purple.

"But, Tim," Samantha says, "no one would COME. We only have the people here at this table to invite. And, I hate to remind you, but people coming to a dance are going to expect GIRLS!"

"Well, we have one on the guest list already," I joke. Samantha just fixes me with a cool stare.

"I'm serious, Tim," she says. "You know how the other kids are going to react to our invitations? They're going to laugh. They're going to say that there's no way the Geeks could ever make a dance cool. And they'll probably even try to ruin it. We'll actually be even worse off than we were before."

"Yeah," Glenn agrees, "and, also, have you thought about all the work we'd have to do? We'd have to, like, ask for permission from the teachers. And how would we get the money to have snacks? My dad is *not* going to let me have extra allowance this month. And also— also, what about music? And decorations?"

"Calm down, Glenn. No need to pop a blood vessel."

Kirk and J.D. are still staring at me in disbelief. Neither has said a word.

"No, but seriously, wait a sec, guys," I say, imitating the tone my dad takes when he explains something on the computer to me. He always takes it slow, with lots of pauses. And he always makes sure to ask if I have any questions. Right now, I need to act like I'm explaining something that seems easy to me to people who think it's hard. "You're getting too focused on the details. Yes, we'll have to worry about all that stuff down the road. But think of it this way. It's like I was saying with the phone thing. Right now we're the lame phones that no one wants. But if we start doing stuff like we're *already* cool, the rest of the school will eventually start to wonder. They'll wonder if we've really been popular all along, but no one knew. Nobody's gonna want to be left out of the cool new group—*us*. And the dance will be how we do it!"

"Well," says Samantha quietly, "I *do* have all that music stored on my laptop."

"And I could probably figure out how to set up speakers," adds Glenn.

"Oooh! And, I know! We'll keep our identities secret until the end! And build up all these rumors about the dance so that people come!" Samantha's ideas are gaining steam.

"Awesome!" Glenn agrees. "I wish I'd thought of that."

"We'll call it . . ." In my head I imagine a drum roll like they have on those late night television shows that I'm not supposed to watch because they're on so late. *Tra-da-da-da-da-da-da-da-da-da-da* . . .

"The Mystery Ball!"

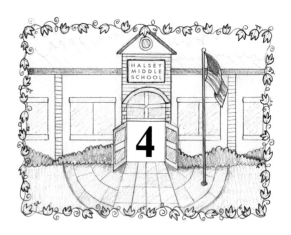

The Mystery Ball
Planning Committee

O VER THE NEXT FEW LUNCH HOURS, WE BEGIN TO GET our plan together. Samantha keeps track of it all on her laptop.

Tim: Ask Mrs. Zuck for help about getting the auditorium. Pick a date. (We picked April 1—April Fool's Day, to be funny.) Fundraise for decorations (I have a highly brilliant plan for taking care of this.)

Samantha: Spread the word with our publicity campaign. Create the dance playlist to end all playlists. Help plan decorations with Glenn.

Glenn: Help Samantha with the publicity campaign. Get some of the popular kids to say they'll go to the dance. Help plan decorations and set up speakers.

The only members of the group who have not offered to help yet are Kirk and J.D. In fact, they even missed sitting at the lunch table one or two times. I'm not sure why, but things are so busy now with planning that I haven't gotten to the bottom of it yet.

I decide to tackle my own to-do list right away. After Computer Resource class one day, I wait for the other kids to leave. Mrs. Zuck has half her head buried in a crate of extension cords, digging around for something. After a bit of talking to herself, she notices I'm there.

"Oh, good. Tim. Just the person I need. Could you look in there for a firewire cord while I get these computers shut down? Thanks, dude." That's one of the things I like about Mrs. Zuck. She sometimes calls people "dude."

"Sure," I say. Even though I find the cord she's looking for almost immediately, I pretend to look around a little more.

"Um, Mrs. Zuck?"

"Yes, Tim?"

"There's this group of people that I know . . . and, well, they need to use the gym."

"Well, great!" Mrs. Zuck says. I can tell she's still distracted by the computers she's shutting down. "They can go fill out a form with Beverly at the front desk. It's a request form. And then the vice principal will look at it and make the decision."

Gulp. Of course it would be Assistant Principal McCloud who gets to decide whether or not we have our dance. Of course. I think back to him in his office saying that we shouldn't "disturb" the school while his weird fish stared at me with her fishy eyes. There's gotta be some way around this.

"Could a teacher submit the request?" I ask. My heart is pounding, but I try to sound *highly* relaxed about the whole thing. I want Mrs. Zuck to think she's helping a group she doesn't even know.

"Well, that depends," she says. "If a teacher is the leader of a group, then yes, she'd be able to submit the request form." *Excellent!*

"This group already has a leader."

"Well, what about a faculty advisor, then? That's a teacher who just meets with students but let's them do their own activities. What IS the group anyway?" she asks.

"The Mystery Ball Planning Committee." The words just burst from my lips.

Mrs. Zuck raises a single eyebrow. "Huh. I've never heard of that one."

"They're new. I know one of them, and I'm helping him, er, *her* create this, um, dance. Hopefully soon."

"I see." Mrs. Zuck leans back on her desk, arms

crossed. I can tell I have her full attention now. "I take it I'll be talking to the group leader through you then?"

"Yep! He—*she* hasn't moved here yet. But she'll be here soon. So, in the meantime . . ."

"Interesting. A student that wants to throw a huge dance for Halsey students she hasn't met yet. *Very* interesting. Well, I've got five more minutes until the next bell, Tim. Tell me about this dance and I might be able to help you with that form."

Success! Objective Number One: Achieved.

I REPORT BACK TO THE GROUP AT LUNCH, AND IT SOUNDS LIKE they've been making good progress, too. Samantha and Glenn show me the sketches they've made of how we will transform the gym. "It will be kind of like deep space," Glenn says.

"Yeah," Samantha agrees. "We're going to use a projector and my older sister's special lights to have a light show."

"And Samantha has already made a huge playlist."

"And then *Glenn* will connect my laptop to his speakers."

I still feel like we're missing something. We want the other students to leave happy, right?

"What about snacks?" I ask. That's what we're missing.

"We could use clear soda with food coloring!" Samantha says. "Everything could be a cool color! Like, um, blue cookies or red popcorn."

I smile at the thought of our table with rows of brightly colored drinks and food. It will be like touching down in the future or something. Plus, everything will match our bright flashing lights. It's going to be *highly* cool. No one will be able to dismiss us as "just geeks" again. Well, hopefully.

"What about the fundraising?" Glenn wants to know.

"That, I need your help with."

So, here's the thing. I knew that if we tried to collect donations as the Geeks throwing a dance, NO

ONE would donate. Or even show up at all. BUT, if everyone thinks they're donating to a mystery dance, they'll be too curious to turn down the chance. We've got to spread rumors in advance about how fun the dance will be. We have to start the other kids guessing about who's behind it. We have to build what my Dad calls "buzz" when he's talking about his work at Zenith. "That product succeeded because it really had a lot of buzz behind it," he'll say. One bee picks up an idea and buzzes it to a flower, who buzzes it to another bee, who buzzes it across the garden. From there, the buzz keeps spreading. So, um, I guess I'm calling Samantha, Glenn, and myself bees. We have to be the bees that begin the buzz about the Mystery Ball.

WE START IN GYM, WHICH IS ONE OF THE ONLY CLASSES THAT the three of us all have together. Gym is pretty much a class designed by one of the evil warlords of Valcora to crush the spirit. Samantha is actually a pretty fast runner and Glenn is decent at dodgeball, but me? I'm terrible at everything. I know, a geek who's bad at sports . . . that's no surprise, right? I guess I just tried to do sports once, when I was *really* little, and I could tell I would never be the best at it. And in case you haven't figured this out about me yet, I sorta like being the best. Whether it's math or after-school drum class or computers. When I'm not the best, I get bummed out. So, I really just avoid things when I know I can't win.

Why am I trying to create a school dance, then? Your guess is as good as mine.

"Think fast, geek!" Joe Russo yells as he whips a basketball at my face. I duck as fast as I can, though I can feel the *Whiz!* of the basketball as it brushes the top of my head. I don't get Joe Russo. I really don't. Mrs. Zuck assigned me to help him with his computer work in class at the very beginning of the year. I help him every day. I'm always patient. Sometimes I think I can almost see a smile forming on his face, or spot a ripple of expression that might mean, "Hey, I appreciate that you've been helping me out every day even though I'm grouchy." I'm never sure what's going through Joe Russo's large head, though. I barely get more than a "nkyou" from him, which in my opinion doesn't qualify as actual speech. And now?! It's like all those times of being nice and helpful mean exactly *zilch.* As soon as we're on HIS turf (the gym), he uses those big beefy arms to throw things right at my head.

I'm used to this—other sixth graders being okay to the Geeks in class and then mean in the halls. But still. It stings. We need Joe Russo to spread the word about the Mystery Ball, though. We need him because of his friends the Football Lardos and the Deadly Sweets. If a guy like Joe Russo says something is going to be cool, other kids listen. Our plan is pretty brilliant, if I do say so myself. In between practicing our free throws and three-point shots, Samantha, Glenn, and I talk in our group. Not loudly, but at the same time, loud enough for the other kids to hear.

"So, *who* are these people throwing a dance at

Halsey School?" Samantha asks me.

"I don't know. *Nobody* knows. I heard an eighth grader saying something about it on the bus." (If an eighth grader says something, it's definitely a lot cooler.) "I guess Assistant Principal McCloud doesn't want them to have it because it might get too out of control."

"What will the music be like?"

"I don't KNOW!" I pretend to be irritated at Samantha. "I was honestly just listening to an eighth grader on the bus. But I guess it's a mystery dance on April first."

I see Joe Russo look my way a couple of times, so I'm pretty sure he's overheard. The seed is planted!

For the rest of the week, the three of us stage these conversations in all sorts of places: in the hallways, by writing mystery notes on the chalkboard, by talking on the bus. We start fundraising, too, by leaving one box out in the lunchroom and one in the sixth-grade common area. "Mystery Dance Fund," we wrote on the boxes. "DONATE HERE!" It takes a few days, but I do see a couple of kids slide one-dollar bills into the boxes' slots when no one's looking. Of course, we have to monitor the boxes closely to be sure that no one gets *too* attached to them.

Plus, Mrs. Zuck tells me after class one day that she has good news. She submitted the request form to the front office and it's been approved! The school will even give us a $25 planning fund, which we can also use for decorations and supplies.

"McCloud gave me a bit of a rough time over not knowing the exact details of who was organizing the dance. But in the end, I vouched for you," she tells me. "I told him that one of my best and most responsible students was involved." Her eyes gleam at me a little. "I just hope my good judgment is not misplaced . . ."

"Oh, definitely not, Mrs. Zuck!" I jump in. "I know these people. I know they'll do a great job planning the dance. They, um, she, is *highly* responsible."

"Well, okay," Mrs. Zuck says, turning to a pile of

papers on her desk. "If you say so!"

I know it's definitely a risk to use a fake identity on the request form. Both for us and for Mrs. Zuck, really. We could have gotten *her* in trouble, I realize, even though I didn't think of that before. Mrs. Zuck must have known that, but she did us the favor of submitting the form in spite of the risk. I can picture McCloud now, muttering to himself and looking suspiciously at the form. Mrs. Zuck must have *really* worked to convince him. That's why she's pretty much the most awesome teacher at Halsey School.

"Seriously, they will be so grateful," I say. Mrs. Zuck gives me a little wink in reply.

"Good luck, dude."

FROM THEN ON, EVERY TIME I PASS MCCLOUD'S OFFICE, I can't help but shudder just a little bit. One word from him and the whole dance is off. After all of our hard work! We have to be sure to keep him as far away from the planning as possible. I'm not sure if the Mystery

Ball could be what he considers a "disturbance," but I

DON'T want to find that out the hard way.

$$COUNTDOWN:$$
$$2 \ WEEKS \ TO \ GO$$

. . .And things are looking (pretty) good.

Betrayed

SO FAR, OUR PLAN IS WORKING PERFECTLY. NO MATTER where you go at Halsey School, *someone* is talking about the Mystery Ball on April 1st.

"I heard that it's, like, the son of a famous actor from England or something. He has to come to school here because he's, like, in *hiding*. Someone told his dad that they would kidnap him if he stayed in England. So he's moving here and is throwing this party to meet new friends. Um, and also? He's going to arrive at the dance in his own helicopter," I hear Stella Sweet tell a whole table of Sweets in the cafeteria.

"I heard that there will be lots of girls there from other schools," Joe Russo tells some other Lardos during gym. They're doing stretches and trying to touch their toes. Only Joe can actually do it; the rest are stuck wiggling their fingers near their knees. "We probably won't even know any of them. But still, I bet they'll be *way* nicer than the stuck-up girls at Halsey."

I even hear rumors about the Mystery Ball from students I don't know. "Pssst!" a random guy in my science class says. "Do you know how I can get a ticket to the Mystery Ball next week?"

YOU KNOW, THEY CALL IT THE "SWEET TASTE OF SUCCESS" for a reason. Having the whole school excited about our dance *does* taste pretty great. Like a Snickers bar straight out of the fridge, or hot cocoa when the whipped cream on top has melted just right. The only bummer about the whole thing is that Kirk and J.D. haven't helped at all. In fact, they almost seem afraid of us now. Whenever we start talking about the dance, they either roll their eyes or start fiddling with their calculators. They sit alone a lot at lunch now, whispering to each other in their own little corner of the cafeteria and looking over their shoulders. I try to go up to J.D. after class and ask him what's going on, but he brushes me off.

"Kirk and I don't want to get involved, okay?" he says, looking nervous. Well, fine. If they don't want to be part of the most interesting event at Halsey School, EVER, then that's *their* loss.

THE DANCE IS GOING TO BE HELD ON A SATURDAY NIGHT, so we got permission (well, the Mystery Ball Planning Committee did, anyway) to set up most of our decorations the night before. Glenn was really into secret codes today. "See you at the *staging area* at *oh-*

four-hundred," he said after we left the lunch table earlier in the afternoon to go to class.

"Glenn, you have to stop this!" Samantha said, laughing. "Nobody has any idea. We're in the clear! But they *will* be suspicious if you keep trying to use secret movie code."

"Well, all I meant," Glenn whispered, "was that I would see you guys at four o'clock in the gym."

"Got it. Over and out, Glenn." Samantha walked away, still laughing. She really can be rude sometimes, but I had to laugh, too. I think, in Glenn's mind, we're all in a top-secret Bond movie or something.

―――――

NOW, WE'RE IN THE GYM WITH A HUGE PILE OF COLORED lights at our feet from Samantha's sister, a laptop, and Glenn's ginormous speakers. After we finish setting up, we're going to go over to my house to make our treats with food coloring. My parents said it would be okay after I told them we were planning an extra credit event about ultraviolet light. With snacks, of course.

Not that I think my parents would blab the truth about the Mystery Ball, but Glenn does have one thing right. When you're doing something top secret, you've got to make sure it stays that way.

Glenn and Samantha get to work connecting the speakers to Samantha's laptop so that we can test the music. I drag the heavy folding tables out from behind the bleachers. After pulling out just two of the tables, I'm definitely sweating and wishing I had a little extra help. As if on cue, Kirk and J.D. walk in. I told them about our plan to help set up earlier in the day, but they both shook their heads.

"Too much homework," J.D. said before they hurried away. Of course, we didn't tell anyone else we'd be setting up, not even Mrs. Zuck. I do have an excuse if someone comes in, though. I will just say that we were hired by the Mystery Ball Planning Committee to decorate and do the sound for the dance. Everyone knows geeks are good at setting up a sound system, right? Sometimes you've gotta play that stuff to your advantage.

"Hey, guys!" I wave to Kirk and J.D. "Perfect timing! I've got to pull like three more of these tables out."

They just stand there, though, not moving or making eye contact with me. Right then, the door bangs again and a squat figure strides in on very quick legs.

Assistant Principal McCloud, his face violet and blotched with anger.

"Thank you, Mr. Kirk, Mr. J.D.," he says, rocking

back and forth on his heels. "I see you were right."

SAMANTHA AND GLENN SNAP TO THEIR FEET. "WHAT'S going on?" Samantha shouts. She takes a couple of angry steps towards Kirk and J.D. They step back as if they're afraid she's going to follow that up with a fist. Glenn shakes his head and crosses his arms.

"I can't believe it, guys," he says, shaking his head again. "I just can't believe you'd do that." It doesn't seem like Kirk and J.D. are feeling too happy with themselves at the moment, either. Both of them wear a pale and sunken expression. They can barely even look at us.

"Sorry, guys," Kirk whispers. "We just have to be careful, ya know? We can't do anything that would affect us getting into college. We can't have something bad on our record."

"Well, the last time I checked, you guys hadn't helped us with the dance at all!" Samantha says, still looking like she might throw a punch.

"Samantha!" Glenn shouts. "Stop!" I know what he means. She's giving us away even more to Assistant Principal McCloud, who's still standing there looking *very* angry. He just keeps rocking on his heels, glancing from my face to Glenn's face to Samantha's face.

As for me? For once, I'm tongue-tied. I know I'm supposed to be the leader of the Geeks and this should be my cue to jump in and smooth things over. I should find a way to sweet-talk Assistant Principal McCloud. I should explain just what we're doing in the gym, while still protecting the Mystery Ball. I should be confident, like I pretended to be when I was last in McCloud's office, even while his fish, Chloe, was staring at me. But . . . I can't seem to find my voice. I just wasn't prepared for two "friends" to give us away to the *one* person who has the power to stop the dance in its tracks.

Is the rebellion over before it even began? What about all the work we've done—getting people excited about the dance, working with Mrs. Zuck, planning?

The whole point was to wow the whole school with the coolest dance ever, and *then* to reveal the truth: The Geeks had planned the whole thing. We were going to change our image, once and for all. We were going to start demanding a little respect. We were going to get some of the good P.R. "buzz" my dad always talks about at work. And now? Standing here with a pile of lights and tables and speakers at my feet, I can feel all those dreams crashing down to the ground. It feels kind of like getting your homework torn in half. Except worse.

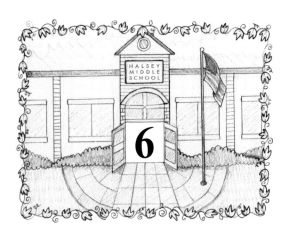

The Mystery Ball

"So, Mr. Watkins, I can see that you took my instructions to *not* create a disturbance at Halsey School and disobeyed them. Completely."

I don't know what's wrong with me, but my tongue feels stuck to the top of my mouth with tape or something. Me? The one who always wants to jump in with the answer? That me is still stuck, unable to speak up.

"I've been told a number of very *interesting* things by these two helpful young men here." McCloud gestures towards Kirk and J.D., who both keep backing up towards the doors of the gym. They're probably trying to make an escape. "They've informed me," he continues, "that the dance, which I approved a month ago is, in fact, organized by YOU. And that you created a fake group . . . for reasons I have not discovered yet. And you even lied to Mrs. Zuck and got her to submit a form for you. Naturally, I have informed her of your actions as well." He shakes his head, and reaches up to scratch his chin with two big fingers.

Now, he turns directly to me. "Mr. Watkins, I just cannot understand why, after your little *roar* incident and after I let you take a pass, you decided to try this charade instead."

I look down, and I hate to admit this, but I feel a hot tear fizzing underneath my eyelashes. This has got to be a low point: crying in the Halsey gym in front of all my friends and the meanest assistant principal in the whole world. I mean, seriously, he's even meaner than some of the monsters in my Valcora game.

"Hey!" someone shouts, interrupting Assistant Principal McCloud. I look up, surprised. McCloud does, too. He looks around like a bird flying off its perch after hearing a loud sound.

It's Glenn and Samantha, standing there looking serious. I'm not even sure which one shouted. Samantha takes a step forward and then Glenn follows. They both stand almost toe-to-toe with Assistant Principal McCloud. He backs up a little bit.

"Mr. McCloud," Samantha says, "we know what this looks like. But all we're trying to do is put on something nice for Halsey School." She gestures to me. "Tim came up with this idea as something we could do as a group. Because we're all friends and, well, we need to help each other."

"Yeah," says Glenn. "Tim knows that you didn't want a disturbance, but we just want the rest of the school to take us seriously. We thought that maybe after this dance, they'd look at us differently. The other kids bother us all the time. We knew we *had* to pretend to be someone else to get them to come."

"If Tim is going to be in trouble, then you better take us to the office, too. The Geeks stand together!" says Samantha, standing tall and puffing out her chest. Glenn pumps his fist. Assistant Principal McCloud looks like he honestly doesn't know what to make of all this. And me? I've never felt so warm and happy in my life. These are *my* friends. And they just stood up for me when I couldn't stand up for myself. I guess you could say I feel *highly* lucky.

"Hmm . . ." Assistant Principal McCloud grumbles. I don't think he likes being in this situation. It kind of makes him look like the bad guy, even if we did make some mistakes. I mean, we *did* lie . . . but it was for a good cause! Now, the gym door creaks open again and Mrs. Zuck walks in.

"Hey, Morty," she calls to McCloud. Morty?! His name is Morty?! Somehow that makes him seem a LOT less threatening.

"Oh, Mrs. Zuck, well, er . . ." He seems at a loss.

I think he still wants to be mad, but part of him just wants to forget about the whole thing.

"Can I make a suggestion?" Mrs. Zuck asks him. "How about instead of detention, we put these three to work in the Computer Resource room. I could use some help after school with working on the networks. I am their faculty advisor, after all." I look over at Mrs. Zuck, almost afraid to meet her eyes, but she makes the tiniest wink back at me. She's on our side!

"Well . . . well . . ." McCloud crosses and uncrosses his arms. Steps forward and then steps back. Finally, he throws his arms dramatically up into the air. "Okay! Make sure you report to me. Tell me if they miss even a single day. I'm serious. One single day."

"Of course," Mrs. Zuck replies calmly.

"I'm a busy man," McCloud says, "and I've got other things to do." He begins to shuffle out of the gym.

"Sir?" I call to him. My voice is finally back. "What about the Mystery Ball?"

McCloud turns back around and wearily waves his arm at me. "Oh, you already have all these . . . things . . . everywhere. And Mrs. Zuck has agreed to chaperone. You might as well go ahead." He sighs heavily and trundles out of the gym once and for all. The three of us all wait for a few seconds and then we're jumping and high fiving and cheering.

"Wahoo! Mission accomplished!" Glenn yells.

Mrs. Zuck is smiling at us, too. "Looks like you guys have a lot of work to do," she says. "Better hop to it."

"Um, Mrs. Zuck, THANK YOU." I try to act like a grown up and shake her hand. She shakes mine firmly back.

"I know what sixth grade can be like," she says with a smile. "But, hey, next time? Let's not make up any fake students, m'kay? Then I might actually have to get mad."

"Deal."

"Deal."

"Deal."

All three of us repeat the word.

———

It's 8 p.m. on the night of the dance. Red popcorn and blue and yellow sugar cookies line the tables. Thirty cups of punch in every shade of the rainbow glitter and bubble. It's dark. Samantha and Glenn and I stand there, hearts beating. Halsey gym doesn't seem quite as gross as usual, even though the wood floor feels sticky under our feet. The smell of sweat from gym class the day before has finally faded. Mrs. Zuck is stationed outside the gym doors, ready to let the first students in. We hear footsteps outside the door.

Creeaaaakkkk.

The door opens.

"Here goes nothing," I say. In unison, I flip on the light show, Samantha presses "play" on her laptop, and we're off! The Mystery Ball has officially begun.

———

The next couple of hours are kind of a blur. At first,

Samantha and I look at each other and whisper, "Uh-oh," because only a few students come in. They look around and see that no one is there and almost leave.

But then, a whole lot of students begin coming in. In wave after wave, they come up to the tables and look at our colored punch. Some of them grab cookies. They stand around, looking up at our blinking light show with wide eyes. They nibble cookies. I see Sweets and Lardos and kids from my classes. I even see some kids I've never actually seen before.

"Cooool lights," I overhear one of the Sweets murmuring. So far, no one has really noticed us, since we're up against the wall near the speakers and laptop.

"Pssst, Samantha!" I whisper.

"Yeah?"

"I think we're going to have to start the dance party ourselves."

"Do we have to?"

"Yep."

"You in, Glenn?" I know Glenn doesn't exactly

love dancing, but teamwork is good, right?

"Okay," he sighs.

The three of us go out onto the dance floor where the bass makes the wood floors shake. We step from side to side and raise our hands in the air. Samantha grins. And what can I say? We dance. At first, it's just us, but whether it's the music or the cool lights, soon, a few other kids shrug and come out onto the dance floor, too. We bounce up and down. I can hear the rubber of my shoes squealing on the wood floors. I feel elbows poking me as other students show off their dance moves.

As more and more kids go out to the floor, I catch sight of Joe Russo from gym and computer class. He's nodding his head to the beat. Suddenly, Kirk and J.D. are there, too. They step out shyly, and seem to search for Samantha, Glenn, and me in the crowd. When they see us, they give us very serious, very sorry nods. And then, even *they* are dancing! I turn back to Glenn and Samantha, and I can't seem to stop smiling. Glenn raises his hand to give us both a high five. I'm pretty sweaty from dancing so much, so it's kind of a slippery high five.

I close my eyes, and for once, I don't think of anything. I'm just lost in the sound of the music and the feeling of my friends dancing next to me.

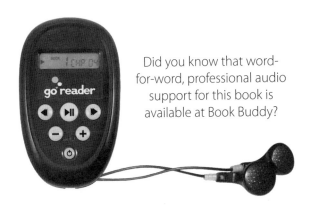

Did you know that word-for-word, professional audio support for this book is available at Book Buddy?

GoReader™ powered by Book Buddy is pre-loaded with word-for-word audio support to build strong readers and achieve Common Core standards.

The corresponding GoReader™ for this book can be found at: http://bookbuddyaudio.com

Or send an email to: info@bookbuddyaudio.com